Albion Winegar Tourgée

A Memorial of Frederick Douglass

Albion Winegar Tourgée

A Memorial of Frederick Douglass

ISBN/EAN: 9783744664394

Printed in Europe, USA, Canada, Australia, Japan

Cover: Foto ©Raphael Reischuk / pixelio.de

More available books at **www.hansebooks.com**

MEMORIAL

OF

FREDERICK DOUGLASS

Yours truly
Frederick Douglass

A

MEMORIAL

OF

FREDERICK   DOUGLASS

FROM THE

CITY OF BOSTON

BOSTON

PRINTED BY ORDER OF THE CITY COUNCIL

MDCCCXCVI

PRESS OF

Rockwell and Churchill

BOSTON

CITY OF BOSTON.

IN COMMON COUNCIL, December 26, 1895.

Ordered, That the Clerk of Committees, under the direction of the Committee on Printing, be directed to prepare and publish an edition of one thousand copies of a volume containing an account of the memorial services in honor of FREDERICK DOUGLASS; the expense attending the same to be charged to the appropriation for City Council, Incidental Expenses.

Passed. Sent down for concurrence. December 30, came up concurred. Approved by the Acting Mayor, January 1, 1896.

A true copy.

Attest:

JOHN M. GALVIN,
City Clerk.

CONTENTS.

PAGE

Death of Frederick Douglass 11

Action of the City Council 15

Memorial Services 19-23

The Eulogy 27-67

Personal Reminiscences 71-90

Final Proceedings 93-94

DEATH OF FREDERICK DOUGLASS

DEATH OF FREDERICK DOUGLASS.

FREDERICK DOUGLASS died at his home in Washington, D.C., on Anacosta Hill, just across the eastern branch of the Potomac River from Capitol Hill, on the evening of the twentieth of February, 1895. The immediate cause of his death was heart failure.

ACTION OF THE CITY COUNCIL

ACTION OF THE CITY COUNCIL.

On the twenty-first of March, Mr. STANLEY RUFFIN, of Ward 9, offered the following order:

Ordered, That a committee of five, with such as the Board of Aldermen may join, be empowered to make arrangements for a public memorial in honor of the late Hon. FREDERICK DOUGLASS; the expense attendant on the same to be charged to the Contingent Fund of the City Council.

The order was concurred in by the Board of Aldermen April first, and approved by the Mayor April third.

The following-named members were appointed upon the Committee, viz.: Aldermen HORACE G. ALLEN, JOHN H. LEE, and EDWARD W. PRESHO, Councilmen STANLEY RUFFIN, MICHAEL T. CALLAHAN, MICHAEL E. GIBBS, CHARLES H. HALL, and J. HENDERSON ALLSTON.

MEMORIAL SERVICES

MEMORIAL SERVICES.

The Committee of Arrangements did not progress sufficiently in their preparations to enable them to hold the memorial services prior to the summer vacation, and consequently were compelled to defer them until fall. They succeeded in securing the services of Hon. ALBION W. TOURGÉE, as eulogist, a gentleman who, on account of his fine literary attainments and intimate acquaintance with DOUGLASS, was peculiarly well fitted for the duty. It was decided to hold the service in Faneuil Hall on the evening of December twentieth. Mr. RICHARD T. GREENER, a long-time friend of DOUGLASS, accepted an invitation from the Committee to give some personal reminiscences of DOUGLASS, and the Dumas Male Quartet was engaged to furnish music for the occasion.

Invitations were sent to the Mayor, City Council, and City officials, to members of the DOUGLASS family, the survivors of the old Anti-Slavery Society, and to many prominent colored people in Boston and vicinity.

The weather was propitious, and the hall was well filled with interested auditors. At the appointed time Chairman ALLEN, of the Committee, took the chair, and the exercises commenced with singing by the quartet "Day Slowly Declining." The Chairman then made the following introductory remarks:

REMARKS OF ALDERMAN ALLEN.

LADIES AND GENTLEMEN. — We are assembled to-night, at the invitation of the City of Boston, to pay a tribute of respect to the life and character of FREDERICK DOUG-LASS. Eminence in any walk of life may well be commended, and in all cases should be appreciated and fittingly recognized; but it is particularly commendable where the goal has been reached after a terrible struggle and in the face of such difficulties as beset Mr. DOUGLASS. Born a slave, in actual want for food, cruelly treated, no one interested in him save with the interest of an owner for a growing chattel, he yet, by perseverance, upright life, and broad-mindedness, became, I may safely say, the most eminent man of his race during the latter years of his life.

It seems also particularly appropriate that this service should be held in Faneuil Hall, Boston, pregnant as it is with historical incidents so important to the race to which he belonged, in whose behalf these walls have echoed the stirring utterances of a PHILLIPS and a GAR-RISON, and of many another earnest and intelligent worker for freedom, for common humanity, and common mankind.

I will ask Rev. Mr. ROBERTS to open the meeting with prayer.

PRAYER BY REV. D. P. ROBERTS.

O Thou Holy One, Thou who art the Author of all being, the Life of all existence, the Spirituality of all spirit, and the Thought of all thinking, Thou High and

Holy One, who inhabiteth not only temples made with hands, but who inhabiteth eternity, we recognize in Thee the Source of our being, the Spring of all our delights, the One to Whom we are accountable and unto Whom we shall render an account for our stewardship here below; that One who presideth not only over the destinies of nations and of worlds, but Who presideth over the destinies of the individual; that One Who hath such a tender regard for the workmanship of His own hand that not a sparrow falleth to the ground without Him.

We thank Thee, Father, that we again come into Thy presence to-night and in this service recognize Thee and Thy hand that hath brought us here. We come, blessed Father, to show our respect to the memory of one whom Thou hast given to this generation, to this century, and to the world.

We thank Thee, blessed Father, to-night, that from depths the lowest in which it is possible for Thy creatures to be found Thou hast made it possible for them to rise. We thank Thee for that height to which men may reasonably aspire, that height to which by perseverance, by energy, and by fidelity, man may attain. We thank Thee for all that Thou hast done for us in creation, in giving unto us this beautiful world as our home, with all its vast resources and possibilities.

We thank Thee, our Heavenly Father, for what Thou hast done for us in Thy Providence, for all along through the ages past Thy footsteps can be traced and Thy handiwork in the affairs of men can be seen.

We thank Thee for what Thou hast done for redemption, for the noble manhood and divinity Thou hast sent to the world in the presence of Thy Son, to teach us those lessons of virtue, mercy, and equality, which God only can impress, in His goodness and spirit, upon the heart and mind of man.

We thank Thee for all the noble characters Thou hast given us in all the ages of the past, and for all the noble character Thou hast given us in the presence of the person whose memory we cherish and whose life we honor. We ask that to-night in all that may be said, proper and due regard and respect may be shown for the memory of that great man whose life and character, whose attainment and personality, evidenced the possibilities of that race from which he came.

We ask Thy blessings, Heavenly Father, on this great city that has sought to do him this honor and whose people have turned out here to-night to show officially their regard for him as a man, as an American citizen, and as one of America's greatest men.

We ask Thy blessings on his dear family, and grant, God, that we all live to emulate his virtues in our own lives, to follow the example he has set, and to square our lives with the rule of justice he has laid out before us.

We ask all these blessings in the name of Christ. Amen.

At the close of the prayer, a response, "Amen," was sung by the quartet.

Then followed a song, "The Plains of Peace," sung by Mr. SIDNEY WOODMAN. The Chairman then introduced the orator of the evening, Hon. ALBION W. TOURGÉE, who delivered the eulogy. He occupied an hour and fifty minutes, but was listened to throughout with unabated interest by his appreciative audience, and at the close he received a hearty outburst of applause.

The solo, "O Rest in the Lord," was then sung by Mr. HODGES, of the quartet.

The Chairman then introduced Mr. RICHARD T. GREENER, as follows:

Chairman ALLEN. — Mr. TOURGÉE has eloquently and interestingly told us of FREDERICK DOUGLASS as he was known to the world. I know it will give you pleasure to listen for a few moments to some personal reminiscences of Mr. DOUGLASS by his intimate and personal friend. Prof. RICHARD T. GREENER.

Mr. GREENER delivered an eloquent and interesting address, which was received with favor by the audience and frequently applauded.

At the close of his remarks, the quartet sang the part song "Lovely Night." The benediction was then pronounced, and the audience dispersed.

THE EULOGY

BY

ALBION W. TOURGÉE

THE EULOGY.

THE life we commemorate to-night was, in some respects, among the most remarkable the world has ever
known. In sharp and swift recurring contrasts it has
never been excelled. In the distance from its beginning to its ending it has rarely been equalled. If a
man's capacity be measured by what he achieved,
FREDERICK DOUGLASS must be ranked among the great
men of a great day; if by the obstacles overcome, he
must be accounted among the greatest of any time.

HISTORICAL PARALLEL.

In all history there is but one parallel of his career, and that one lacks the most important element.
Twenty-five hundred years ago a slave so won upon
his master's love and pride that he was set free.
The most cultivated people in ancient history hung
upon his words in admiration. Their philosophers imi-
tated his methods; their poets parodied his fables. He
became the friend, counsellor, and ambassador of the
greatest king of his time. When he died Athens voted
him a statue, and four cities claimed the honor of
being accounted his birthplace. He is said to have
been a hunchback, and this fact is always cited as

evidence of his transcendent genius because of the added burthen it imposed. He had not only to overcome the prejudice attaching to his station, but also the aversion inspired by his uncouthness. The schoolboy of to-day, as he cons this story, wonders how he could rise to such heights in the face of such obstacles, especially among a beauty-loving people like the Athenians.

Yet, what were the difficulties in the way of Æsop compared with those which Douglass overcame? What was Grecian bondage in comparison with American slavery? What was Æsop's hump when compared with Douglass' color, considered as an obstacle to personal success? What was the patronage of Crœsus to the friendship of Lincoln and Grant, Sumner and Garrison, Whittier and Phillips — and all the unnumbered host of good men and women to whom Douglass' name became a household word and in whose homes he was a welcome guest? No slave was ever before so potent in the counsels of freemen. No negro ever before became so widely and favorably known among an Anglo-Saxon people.

CONTRASTED WITH ÆSOP.

Æsop was freed from bondage by the favor of his master; Douglass, through the admiration of thousands of dwellers in another land who had heard his voice and wondered at his words while yet a slave, and gladly gave their money to melt the shackles of American barbarism that fettered his limbs and galled his free spirit.

Æsop became the ambassador of a sovereign, Douglass the plenipotentiary of two republics.

Athens gave Æsop a statue because of his wit; DOUGLASS was honored because of the services he had rendered a great nation.

Three classes of the American people are under special obligations to him: the colored bondman whom he helped to free from the chains which he himself had worn; the free persons of color whom he helped to make citizens; the white people of the United States whom he sought to free from the bondage of caste and relieve from the odium of slavery.

As it was meet that Athens, the home of wit, should vote Æsop, the most illustrious of ancient slaves, a statue when he died, so it is most fit, that "in the cradle of liberty," his life should be commemorated who while yet a slave became renowned throughout the world as a champion of freedom. Every citizen of the United States is a debtor to his memory: — every colored man because he relieved them, by his admirable exemplification, from the curse of incapacity which had been put upon them, as an excuse for slavery; and every white man because he did so much to take away the shame that rested on the Republic. The material ills of slavery affected chiefly the colored race; its moral blight was shared by the white people of the country as well. The wrongs of slavery attached to the colored man; its shame rested wholly with the white man. So the obligation of gratitude for its extinction is not a one-sided matter, and it is especially appropriate that Boston, the birthplace of two great revolutions for the promotion of liberty, should be the first American city to do honor to a colored man for his services to the nation which had condemned him and his people to hopeless bondage.

The chief merit that attaches to the people of the North in the great conflict in which slavery perished. consisted not in the fact that we fought for the Federal Union or resisted its disruption; but in the far nobler fact that we fought for liberty — the liberty of a poor. weak. despised people. The tramp of our legions was in tune with that most glorious of national anthems :

> "As He died to make men holy.
> Let US die to make men FREE!"

So. too. the slave who fought for his own freedom. in the field or in that great conflict that came before the sword was drawn. fought also to take away the shame of the oppressor. He who fights for his own liberty is a hero; he who strikes a blow for another's rights is the brother of Him who died for man. and fit to wear Excalibar.

A FIRST MEETING.

Some forty years ago a country lad sat in an audience which an orator was addressing in impassioned tones, on an unpopular theme. The speaker was in the prime of manhood. His dark cheek flushed. his eyes flashed; his lithe but powerful frame swayed with the force of his emotion as he denounced wrong and pleaded for justice. Suddenly one of the shafts of his denunciation struck deeper than the others. There was a murmur of disapproval swelling to an angry roar. and then a storm of groans and hisses. From the neighborhood of the

youngster an egg was thrown which struck the speaker
on the shoulder. Other missiles were thrown also, but
this one splashed up on his long wavy hair and left
yellow streaks on his black beard and mustache. There
was an instant's hush broken only by the boy's laugh.
Then for half an hour that audience were thrilled and
hushed to breathless silence, by an overwhelming tide of
denunciatory eloquence rarely equalled in any age or by
any orator. The speaker evidently thought the youngster who laughed had been guilty of the offence. Others
thought so, too. It is not the first time a laugh has
condemned the innocent. The next morning the young
man called upon the orator to apologize, not for the
egg, of which he was guiltless, but for the laugh, which
he regretted. It was not a pleasant call. The orator
was still sore over the indignity that had been offered
him. The affront was one apologies could not cure.
He told the wondering boy a furious tale of insults
he had suffered because he was a colored man pleading
for justice to his people. The interview ended peace-
fully, however, as if in apology for its rough beginning.

A PLEASANT ACQUAINTANCE.

This was my first meeting with FREDERICK DOUGLASS.
It was the beginning of a pleasant but desultory
acquaintance. When we next met, the flood of battle
had swept away the legal estate of slavery. I was a
dweller in a southern state, he was my guest. Around
us were scattered the fragments of a disrupted social
and economic system — a slave-civilization to which
men were trying to fit the garments of liberty. The

result was grotesque — it is still grotesque. Wise theo-
rists made it a scarecrow, and those who had little
comprehension either of liberty or justice as the heritage
of the colored man, have shred away the patches and
left it a ghastly skeleton. He was seeking in wonder
and amaze to penetrate the future and read the destiny
of his people. He had known two phases of American
life in the slave-republic — the slave-life into which he
was born; the free life to which he had fled. How to
reconcile the fragments of the one with the triumphant
confidence of the other was the problem that confronted
all. He knew what had been in the old slave-epoch;
the young man realized more keenly, perhaps, the character of the new one. Neither was confident of what
would be. From that time until just before his death,
we met occasionally as our paths crossed, here and there.
Our acquaintance was always candid, earnest, thoughtful
— never continuous or intimate. I shall speak of him
to-night, therefore, not as one having special knowledge
of those qualities which appear only in personal relations,
but as a public man in his relations to the epoch in
which he lived, the institution he helped to overthrow,
the race whose obloquy he bore, the nation he helped
to redeem from ignominy, and the people whose destiny
he left unsolved. I shall consider only the man whom
the world knows, in the light the future must regard
him.

THE THOUGHT THAT UNDERLIES A LIFE.

Emerson has noted the value of the man who stands
behind a thought. There is also a value to be esti-
mated of the thought that lies back of a man's life,

Every man is, in a sense, chameleonic. He gives back, more or less clearly, the color of his day. If he is careful only of his own comfort or seeks only his own advantage, he reflects but little of the life which is the light of his world. Its rays fall upon him and glance off without any added flash or fresh throb of interest. If, however, its glare enters his soul, fires his brain, and animates his being, he becomes transparent, like the little creature whose flesh absorbs the sunshine so that we see his heart-beats through the glowing walls.

This was true in an especial manner of the man we are assembled to commemorate. The thought of his epoch was *his* thought — he had little outside of or beyond it. From the past he had received only life as his inheritance. His present had nothing to offer but one dominant, controlling idea. This entered his soul and filled it. No wonder: the thought of his time was of himself — himself and his fellows and liberty — their relations to the dominant class in the land of his birth, to the State, to the government, to Christianity, to God. In the church, on the rostrum, in the Congress, in the Legislatures of the country, in the city mart, and in the country store — wherever men were assembled — the one object of all-absorbing interest was the colored man, his character, qualities, capacity, and the relations which God and nature designed that he should hold to his fellow-mortals of a lighter hue. In a sense, this was no new question. The only new thing about it was that there were those who contended that the theory which had so long prevailed in regard to it was not the true one; that the wisdom of the ages was not only incorrect, but that its conclusions were incontestibly based on false premises.

SLAVERY AND CIVILIZATION.

Four hundred years before, Prince Henry, of Portugal, the grandson of that English John of Gaunt whose blood flows in the veins of every monarch of to-day, received a grant from the Roman Pontiff authorizing him, among other things, to seize and hold in captivity as many as he saw fit of the black heathen who inhabited the region which lay beyond the terrible Cape Non, which his caravels had finally passed in safety, in order that they might be taught the principles of the Christian faith and, by and by, be sent back to win over that realm of marvel and mystery, the "Land of the Black-amoors," to the religion of Christ and obedience to Mother Church. The Father of Discovery — the man whose labor and learning, patience and devotion, made Columbus a possibility — was, also, the father of African slavery, made such by his zeal for the religion of which he was a sincere and faithful devotee.

From that time forward, the Church, almost regardless of name or sect, was the guardian and protectress of the traffic in human bodies; all the time with the professed purpose of saving human souls. It came at length to be the accepted theory that the mystery of redemption for Africa lay in the forced migration of the Negro to the slave-republic of the New World, whence, after a time, he was to be returned, Chris-tianized and outworn, to carry the gospel absorbed in bondage, taught by enforced adultery, and exemplified by wholesale robbery and inconceivable oppression, to enlighten the spiritual darkness of Africa. Even yet the pulpit echoes with soul-cheering explications of the divine mystery by which the supernumerary African in our land is to be driven across the sea, to hold up the banner of the Cross and bring the knowledge of the religion of justice and love to them that sit in darkness, leaving this land of liberty to the *exclusive* enjoyment of those for whom it was created and on whom it was divinely bestowed — the white men, who are openly or impliedly proclaimed the worthiest and most favored sons of God.

The doctrine seems a little strange to-day. When FREDERICK DOUGLASS was born, it was a universally accepted truth which was stamped upon his soul in the very instant that he drew the breath of life. It was a slave's breath — the first of a caste-cursed life! The religious and political world have swung forward into a new realm of spirituality and justice, largely through his efforts and the effect of his exemplification of the wrong and shame of the past. We might have endured the wrong which others suffered, but the shame we had ourselves to bear was too much for a sensitive people to endure. For the Yankee is the most sensitive type of humanity; consequently the most chameleonic. He changes quicker and oftener than any other people in the world's history; is sincerely grateful as each Thanksgiving Day comes round that he is not as he was; but has not even yet learned to openly thank God for the fact that he is white. Yet,

next to life and health a white skin is the greatest
blessing that has been enjoyed on American soil since the
Dutch lugger landed the first dusky cargo at Jamestown.
We are destined some time to be as ashamed of caste
based on color, as we are now ashamed of slavery based
on caste. Whether it will require two centuries and a
half to overthrow this monster, as it did destroy its
fellow, Heaven only knows.

HIS INHERITANCE.

Three-quarters of a century ago, or thereabouts, the
child who grew to be the man we call FREDERICK
DOUGLASS was born on a Maryland plantation. He never
knew the date. Years afterward he said, "I am seventeen;" and on that assumption counted the future mile-
stones of his life. Slavery had robbed him even of a
birthday.

Who was his father? None knew. The law forbade
marriage to such as his mother was. Marriage is a
contract; and the slave could make no contract. Such
was the law! A slave could have no will, no power of
self-disposition, no right of person or possession. So this
child had no father and no name. The law of a Christian
land denied to him a legal name as well as legal parentage.
Among the millions of slaves there was not a single husband; not a legal wife; not a parent who had a parent's
right; not a child who could inherit a father's name. Jim,
or Jack, or Joe was all the appellation a slave could bear.
A name imputed family; and Christian civilization denied
the family relation to the slave. "Marriage cannot exist
between slaves" was the deliberate judgment of the

Supreme Court of every slave-state. This was a child to whom the past gave only life; to whom the present brought only such joys as come with health and sense; to whom the future offered — nothing. He was a slave, whom the law defines as "a person without rights;" whom reason defines as a human being deprived of selfhood, opportunity, hope, and ambition (which is based on hope) for the profit and pleasure of another. The law decreed that this child should never have a name, a home, a wife, a child; should never learn to read or write; should never speak to one of the dominant race save hat in hand; should never meet more than two of his fellows for counsel unless a white man was present; should never utter a word of remonstrance, or strike a blow in self-defence or for another's rights, against a man with a white skin!

We shudder at such doctrines now. When this child was born, they were the almost unquestioned beliefs of the American people. No; not unquestioned. There were those who doubted, some that feared, and a few who denied that slavery was either righteous or divine. But they who uttered such denials were accounted guilty of treason and sacrilege; enemies of country, society, and God! This nameless man-child made himself a name; helped to liberate a people; was honored by a great nation; and to-night we meet to commemorate his virtues. Were ever so many miracles crowded into a single life?

A HOPELESS PROSPECT.

Fate hung about the young child's neck two burdens, either of which might well suffice to break the spirit of the strongest man — he was a slave, and bore the

mark of African blood in a nation of Protestant white
people, boastful of their liberty. Either of these curses
was enough to crush hope out of the bravest heart.
Made slaves at birth, how few of our children would
break their fetters! Given a trace of color, how few of
our greatest men would ever have been heard from! It
needs something more than talent, and learning, and
eloquence to open the door of success to a colored man,
and make him welcome on the platform, in the clubs,
and in the homes of men who count their hue a mark
of divine and exclusive favor. If, at the Christmas-tide
which is so near, the Holiest should come again, in hue
and likeness of a negro, even if the heavenly radiance
still shone about His head. I fear me He would meet a
very chilly welcome in the churches and homes of our
land. Clad in a colored integument, there lives not to-day
a single man who could attain to the highest eminence
in our government, or receive a call to a fashionable
church, — no matter what his attainments or how Christ-
like his character! What, then, shall we say of the
prospects of the young child about whose gum-tree cradle
the twin pythons of Slavery and Caste reared their
horrid heads, twined, and hissed to drive away his hope
and dissipate even the dream of aspiration? How shall
we measure his success and estimate his power?

I said he had neither father nor mother. Even the
poor shred of motherhood that slavery left possible was
denied him. He was reared, like any domestic animal, in
the manner best suited to the master's profit; as one of
a family of nondescripts known as "pickaninnies." The
dam was allowed to visit him now and then for his

nutrition; then wholly excluded, and he was removed
to a distance from her.

Once only, in the silence of a summer night, he had
a dream of one who came to the rude pallet where he
slept, knelt beside him, folded him in her arms, and
covered his face with tears and kisses. He knew she
was his mother, though he hardly knew her name, —
the single name she was allowed, — and would scarce
have known her face had he seen her by day. But he
did not see her by day. Long before the dawn she fled
in terror lest she should not be able to repass the nine
long miles that lay between her and the home of him
to whom her service and labor was due, before the day
should come. He never saw her, never heard her voice
or felt her kiss again. Slavery and caste held him in
their clutches as he grew to man's estate.

SLAVE-LIFE.

His slave-life was not remarkable. He changed
masters once or twice; was accounted irritable, if not
discontented and dangerous; tried to break into the
Temple of Knowledge and decipher its mystic scrolls;
learned a trade, and became a skilled worker. Finally
the time came which he was wont to refer in inspired
moments as his "second birth," when he was born, not
into liberty, but into a life where the shackles did not
all the time chafe his limbs. As at his previous birth
he had not been allowed a name, so now, being without
father or mother, he christened himself. It was no
slight testimony to his strength of mind and pertinacity
that he dared to plan and effect his escape from bondage

into that condition of half-liberty which he found in
New England. It was evidence of the character and
quality of his genius that the name he chose was at
once strong, distinctive, and pleasing. That another had
borne it was no matter; it was his by free choice,
having all the names of the earth to choose from. He
did not seek to borrow fame, nor exalt himself by
another's renown. The slave atom did not ask a staff
for his feet, but a symbol for his manhood.

Seventeen years, more or less, FREDERICK DOUGLASS
was a slave. Rough fare, enforced toil by day and
rest by night, had ministered to his bodily development. Slavery was a hard mistress, but she nourished
tough thews. As for his mind, he had mastered a
few letters and formed a desperate resolution. Trained
in those arts of simulation which slavery taught to
every pupil who had aptness enough to learn, he
toiled and waited, not " for something to turn
up " — there was nothing of the Micawber in his
nature — but for the door of opportunity to open even
the least before him. When that time came, he fled
through it to the protection some of the Northern
States tried to give those who dwelt within their
borders. Five years afterwards, the Supreme Court of
the United States decided that such attempted security
was vain.

American slavery was the greatest crime of the
ages: first, because of its utter hopelessness; and,
second, because the intelligence and inventiveness of
the American people had been applied to the refine-
ment and perfection of the legal relations of the

slave, until there was literally no chance for the palliation or amendment of his condition. The State could make him free indeed. This had been done in five of the original colonies. That curious piece of legislation by which slavery was excluded from the Northwest Territory, had saved the whole region west of Pennsylvania and east of the Mississippi, from the contamination of its presence, though even here it held sway over men's hearts and minds. The nation was kept half-free and half-slave by the most nicely adjusted system of checks and balances the ingenuity of man has ever devised. Slavery being based on race and color, the presumptions of the law in favor of liberty were reversed to secure its perpetuity, and the teachings of religion were made the cloak for legalized violation of all the laws of God and nature. While the half-free North had rid herself of Slavery, Caste held sway throughout its length and breadth. Equality of opportunity, which is the touchstone of liberty, was denied to all having traces of colored blood.

THE ABOLITION EPOCH.

Almost contemporaneous with the "second birth" of the slave, thereafter for all time to be known as FREDERICK DOUGLASS, the American people began to awaken to the enormity of that greatest of all crimes against God and man, American slavery.

The New England Anti-Slavery Society had been organized five years before the foot of DOUGLASS touched free soil; the national society, a year or two later,

Garrison had established the "Liberator," and was beating it into the hearts of men with palpitant strokes, that slavery was the sin of sins, and crime of crimes. Phillips had just dedicated the powers which were to thrill the world, to the cause of human liberty and righteousness. Whittier was tuning the harp whose lays were to make him for all ages the prophet-poet of Liberty. Birney had already begun that career which was to drive him from his southern home. Garret Smith was preaching liberty in that strange confusion of rich metaphor, overflowing kindness, and inconsequent conclusion, which marked him one of the worthiest and strangest of patriots and philosophers. Elijah Lovejoy had just given up his life for liberty, and Owen, kneeling on his brother's grave, had just vowed eternal war against Slavery. Thousands more, bursting the green withes of prejudice, were pressing forward, eager to give life and strength to the conflict of freedom. Boston was the storm-centre, for here the fiery heart of Garrison sent forth the flaming sheets which flew over the whole land and, in every home they entered, kindled a fire, which nor time nor tyranny could ever smother. Even yet, thousands of hearts glow and flutter in breasts, now weak and shrivelled, at the memory of his utterances. The ferment had begun which was to culminate in years of strife and bloody expiation — a struggle not yet ended!

DOUGLASS, still in bonds, caught the echoes of this conflict. He had the slave's fear of being thrust back into the Gehenna from which he had fled. He had the slave's intuition that his safety lay in silence and obscurity. For years, he looked with apprehension in the face of every white stranger whom he met, fearing he might bear the warrant for his arrest as a fugitive. By night and by day, the nightmare of recaption and reënslavement followed him. He was determined to die rather than submit. He had muscles of iron, health, and strength. Slavery, harsh mother as she was, had trained him well for self-support. Should he labor in silence, win enough for his wants, and let obscurity ripen into safety? Or should he risk his own liberty to help bring his race the Jubilee — the hour of deliverance from bondage — long prayed for? No one could have blamed him if he had remained silent. The hand of the master reached to every corner of the land. Some of the States remonstrated, but the nation upheld his right.

It was no trivial matter, even for a white man, in New England to espouse the cause of liberty. Society frowned upon him; the pulpits fulminated against him. On that first year of DOUGLASS' semi-freedom, even the Thanksgiving sermons in Boston reeked with denunciation of the crime and sin of obeying the scriptural behest to " Proclaim liberty throughout the land unto all the inhabitants thereof!" American slavery had no year of jubilee, and was far behind that Jewish bondage of twenty centuries before, in humane and merciful character. It not only pursued the fugitive slave to the uttermost borders of its jurisdiction, but it persecuted those who aided him to escape or even claimed for him the more tolerable condition of a " free man of color."

DOUGLASS might, with general approval, have remained in obscurity, won a reasonable competence by his labor, and enjoyed as much liberty and respect as was attainable by the "free person of color" anywhere in the United States. Many had won a precarious liberty in like manner, and kept it by silence. They were not to be blamed. Not only is self-preservation the first law of nature, but the inheritance of slavery does not incline one to sacrifice for others. The slave's peril, privation, and the dwarfing effect of generations of enforced ignorance and restraint but poorly fitted the slave for self-sacrifice for the good of others, let alone the succor of his fellows. There were some who took the same risk and adopted the same course as DOUGLASS, but more who sought safety in the obscurity which soon became insufficient to conceal his identity. He went to an "Abolition meeting." He heard the woes of the slave related by those who knew them not, except through imagination and hearsay. To him the horrors of slavery stood out in all their naked enormity. He had never spoken to an audience before; that night he rose and, begging pardon for his weakness, set forth in a clearer light than any one present had ever heard it told, the horror of that bondage from which he had fled.

DOUGLASS AN ABOLITION ORATOR.

Those engaged in the abolition movement were earnest people. They did not shrink from the logic of their own teachings. They welcomed the new worker in the struggle they had undertaken as having something

they had not — a concrete knowledge more potent with
average minds than the most clearly woven theory.
They noted, too, the fire of genius under his unprepar-
edness. "From night to night," said one, "I watched
the growth of his vocabulary and the fuller play of
his imagination. It was marvellous!"

He was an orator by natural inclination. There
was a rumor that his father might have been one
who "swayed the listening Senate" with his honeyed
words. It matters not whence it came, the natural
aptitude cannot be denied, and the school where he was
put in training was one never excelled in the world's
history. It was the golden age of American oratory —
its most earnest, impassioned, and characteristic epoch.
Of the masters of eloquence of that time many of
the most accomplished were already enlisted, and others
were being daily enrolled among the Abolition forces.
No wonder that DOUGLASS' natural powers were so
swiftly developed that he was soon proclaimed "a most
marvellous orator, when one considers what the life was
from which he came." Under such masters, and with
such a theme, one must have been dull indeed not to
have felt the glow of inspiration!

He had two great advantages over those with whom
he wrought — little was expected of him by his first
audiences, and he was a living refutation of the
charge that his people were incapable of civilization
and fit only for servile tasks.

The question of the colored man's capacity was the
most important premise in the argument which occupied the universal thought. Politics and religion;

business and science; society and economics — all were
colored with the pros and cons of this subject. The
right and wrong of slavery was held to depend upon
it. If the negro was incapable of civilization, slavery,
though an ugly thought, must be endured for the
common welfare and security. On the other hand, if
he was capable of even approximate attainment with
the white race, slavery became at once a monster of
too horrible a mien to be contemplated with anything
like forbearance or approval. Volumes were written
upon the subject. Science and theology went hand
and hand in the service of slavery. Wrong has ever
been a good paymaster, and slavery paid him who
proclaimed its sanctity, and him who upheld its necessity alike, with honors and approval. So the most
noted scientists avouched the negro's inferiority, basing
their judgments upon the curl of his hair, the breadth of
his nose, and the hue of his skin, the convolutions of his
brain, the flatness of his foot! The pulpit used these
demonstrations to prove the wisdom and mercy of God in
fastening on the sons of Ham the curse of the drunken
patriarch. There were lots of loop-holes in the reason-
ing of both; but they both proved what was wanted,
and were accounted oracles in their day. So science and
religion became the willing servants of Slavery and cast
the cloak of duty and necessity over its unutterable in-
famies. Everybody who was of any consequence formed
and expressed an opinion on this engrossing subject
Every lawyer, every statesman, every politician, every
divine, almost every man and woman of any prominence
in the land, was drawn into the vortex of controversy in

regard to the negro's capacity for civilization and the resulting question as to whether he should be free or slave. What tomes of wasted learning were put forth! What ingenious theories were invented to reconcile God's mercy with man's depravity! How many a grandson would be glad to-day to obliterate the evidence of an ancestor's folly! But what is writ, what is printed, can never be recalled. Brass may melt and marble crumble, but printer's ink endureth forever and ever! O scientist! O bigot! if you wish to learn humility and avoid the shame of the world's ridicule, read the record of your predecessors of only fifty years ago, and see how feeble is the wisdom of man when he seeks to put bounds to the mercy and justice of God! Many a man in that day made swift shipwreck of a fair renown in seeking to wrest God's truth to the devil's service. The vast majority of the people, even of the North, were against the negro's right to be free, and that opposition was based almost wholly upon a profound and sincere conviction of his unfitness for civilization and lack of capacity for freedom and self-direction and control.

The Attorney-General of the Commonwealth of Massachusetts, if I mistake not, about that time declared, perhaps in this historic hall, that "one might as well talk about releasing the wild beasts in the Zoölogical Garden to run about the city's streets as think of freeing negroes to prey upon the white people of the country."

Under these circumstances, it was of vast importance to the Abolition movement to have one who in himself

was an undeniable refutation of this claim. Nobody
could question the ability of FREDERICK DOUGLASS.
He was an opponent whom any man had need beware
of, and no champion of slavery cared to encounter
him a second time. While he studied carefully the
eloquence of others and assimilated with amazing readi-
ness the best thoughts and the most striking arguments of his co-laborers, they came forth from the
laboratory of his fiery brain essentially modified and
not seldom greatly improved. From the first, he had
the self-possession of the natural orator. An audience
inspired him; interruptions only brought fresh corrus-
cations. His humor was heightened by an artful assumption of the slave's humility, and, scathing as was his
denunciation, he had a way of excusing it because of his
race and lack of preparation, that somehow deprived it of
offence. Even insult, he turned back on the offender in
a way that not only made him the subject of general
laughter, but not seldom transformed into the insulter
a champion and defender. So he not only rose to
the rank of one of the most noted champions of
liberty, but he became also one of the strongest arguments of all those who fought beside him. Within a
decade he had become one of the most popular of Abolition orators. Many times he was listened to with
patience and applause, when a white orator could hardly
make himself heard because of the hisses and jeers of
unfriendly audiences. Yet there were times when the
very reverse was true, and noble women showed their
courage and devotion to liberty, by gathering around
him and with their persons shielding him from the

wrath of mobs whose only answer to his irrefutable argument was the cry, "Kill the nigger!"

For a dozen years before the war of words grew silent in the clash of arms, it may be doubted if there was any more effective speaker in the Abolition host. His arguments had not the polish of many others; they were not so generally reported by the press, because his efforts were almost always extemporaneous in form, and the stenographer was not then omnipresent; but there was a life, a fire, a personal magnetism about him, which made even the most polished oratory seem weak and vain beside his fiery onslaught.

I was a lad of a dozen years, or less, when I first heard him at a meeting where some of the most eloquent of the white champions of liberty had also spoken. On the way home a crowd of thoughtful country people, of varying opinions, were discussing what they had heard. One of the most intelligent, a leader in his neighborhood, said:

"Well, you may say what you please about the others; the 'nigger' settled it with me. When a Negro who has been a slave can make such a speech as that, it is time that every one of them should be free. I am against slavery from this day."

And he kept his word.

During this time Mr. DOUGLASS became the one colored man who was well and favorably known to the whole American people. At that time, the country-people represented the heart of American sentiment. Only one-fifth of the population lived in great cities, instead of fifty-eight per cent. as now. Throughout all

the country regions of the North the colored man was
rarely seen. There were whole counties without a single
colored inhabitant. Now and then, a fugitive struggled
into a community, and settled down. But in the main,
sentiment of the North in regard to the Negro was based
on hearsay; and very queerly, in this case, the hearsay
of the interested planter was generally preferred over
the testimony of the disinterested observer. To this mass
of opinion, Mr. DOUGLASS came as a concrete fact of
tremendous force. Almost every one spoke kindly and
pleasantly of him; thousands took him into their homes,
and made him the basis of their conclusions in regard
to the righteousness of Slavery. In a dozen States he
had come to be known to a large proportion of the
people, who had little if any knowledge of any other
colored man. When the time came, he was naturally
looked upon as the embodiment of all his race's
interests and qualities.

AS A POLITICIAN.

With the organization of the Republican party in
1854, Mr. DOUGLASS became at once an active and
honored member. This appears the more remarkable
when we consider the fact that there were no colored
voters of any consequence at the North who could be
said to constitute what might be termed a "following"
of his own people. The "free person of color," though
he could not be a citizen of the United States, nor a
citizen of any State, within the meaning of that term
in the Constitution of the United States, by a singular
inconsistency, could be a voter in any State which saw

fit to give him the ballot, and could thus become a part of the electoral power of the nation. This power was, however, conferred on him by only four or five States of the Union, and in these the colored population was very small, and the Republican majorities very reliable. So that, in fact, there was no colored vote which it was of any material consequence to the new party to secure. Besides that, the plain interest of the colored voter has always lain with the Republican party, since through that he has obtained all the rights he has enjoyed, and to that he must still look to secure their enjoyment.

It cannot be said, therefore, that Mr. DOUGLASS was welcomed to the councils of the Republicans because of any influence he had among those of his own race or color whose votes the new party desired to secure. The simple truth is, that he was welcomed as an orator of singularly convincing power, and as a living justification of the party tendency, if not its avowed purpose. He was the first instance of a colored man being regarded as an important factor of a national party, that party being composed entirely of white voters.

As a politician, Mr. DOUGLASS was always cautious and practical. He believed in the theory that every man should use his power as a citizen to secure as much actual betterment as possible, instead of refusing to exercise it unless he could obtain, at once, all that he desired. Had he been a white citizen of Massachusetts, with the advantages of opportunity and education her sons have so long enjoyed, I have no doubt he would have been one of her most noted political leaders. The fact that he broke away from those with whom he had been so long associated, and gave his allegiance to the Republican party because, though not professing a purpose to abolish slavery, it did evince a most earnest purpose to restrict it, is a fine illustration of the intensely practical character of his mind.

"To such a cause as ours," he said, "a little *done* is worth more than ages of clamor about what *ought to be done!*"

It was this quality which eminently fitted him for the role of the practical statesman. He did not originate policies nor invent methods, but he had an unerring instinct as to what promised to advance the cause nearest his heart and bring the public sentiment ultimately to entertain and indorse his plea for liberty and justice for his people. This he always kept steadily in view. Until the emancipation of the slave, politics meant nothing to him except as it bore upon that event. Very many of the leaders of the Abolition movement had imbibed the common fallacy that the only way to secure a needed reform in a republic, is to demand that all other political questions shall be subordinated to it. Mr. DOUGLASS, with a political instinct which seems marvellous now, when we consider the entire exclusion of all other interests from his thought and purpose, recognized the broader fact that a minority should always strive not merely to overcome or force a majority to yield to *all* their demands upon any subject. but to persuade them, if possible, to accept *some* of them. The tact, patience, and knowledge of human nature which he manifested at this period of his career. prove conclusively the eminence he would have attained had not

caste thrown an insuperable barrier in his way. Given
a white skin, and there is no limit to be placed on the
political success he might have achieved.

RELEASE FROM BONDAGE.

There is something very curious in the fact that
FREDERICK DOUGLASS remained for years a slave even
after he had achieved no little eminence as a public
speaker and had become especially distinguished as an
Abolition orator. He was by no means lacking in business capacity, and he must have been in receipt of a
fair income during this period. Why he or his friends
in the North did not raise the insignificant sum necessary to set his mind at rest and save him from the
constant fear of recapture and reënslavement, instead
of waiting for two English women to collect and forward to his owner the very moderate sum requisite to
set him free and relieve him from such apprehension,
I have always been unable to understand. It has been
said that some were so opposed to recognizing the claim
of property in man that they refused to countenance
any such proceeding, and that there were others who
thought his capture and rendition as a fugitive slave
would have such an effect upon the public sentiment
of the North as to advance the cause of liberty even
more than his ceaseless labors as an agitator could.
Of all these things I speak not from personal knowledge. Except the progress of public sentiment which
a boy notes even better than a man, I knew nothing
of the Abolition movement until it entered on its last
stage and became not distinctly a separate movement.

but part of a great national impulse. But hearing him relate his profound emotion at being made entirely a free man — how he went out and walked the streets saying to himself as a strange face appeared :

"I am not afraid! I am free, and no power can tear me from my home or send me back to bondage!"

Hearing him speak of the rapture of this release from the bondage of apprehension, I have wondered that he should have counted it a duty, or that others should have regarded it as a case in which he should have been allowed to suffer for so long a time rather than recognize even by his deliverance the doctrine of property in man.

I have been told very recently, indeed, that he stoutly opposed any such project, and would have forbidden it when set on foot in England had it been in his power. There is no reason to doubt this statement. Indeed, it furnishes the only reasonable solution of the situation, and raises him to the position of a hero, offering his liberty and life to promote the liberation of his people.

Yet it seems hardly in accord with the severely practical quality of his mind, and can only be accounted for upon the fact that individual property in man was then accounted the most essential quality of slavery. In truth, the legal condition of inferiority was, as time has shown, the most important feature of the legal estate of slavery. But whatever the fact, we may be sure that the desire to promote the cause of liberty lay at the bottom of this refusal to buy or to be bought; since those who gave their hearts and hands to the Abolition movement were not the men and women to

permit any other consideration to restrain them from
giving liberty to such a devoted co-worker in the cause.
Indeed, I have no doubt that a penny collection set
on foot among the American people would very soon
have yielded enough to have purchased his liberty, and
for one, I am sorry to-night that this opportunity was
not accorded to them, and the honor of freeing the
most distinguished American slave was permitted to fall
to the lot of the English friends of liberty. No doubt
the course adopted was well-meant ; perhaps it was
wise, but I would have been glad to hand the message
down to my descendants, that I had given even a penny
to take the badge of servitude from the neck of one
who did so much to wake the conscience of the nation
to the shame which was dragging it down to deserved
ignominy.

THE FIRST LEADER OF HIS RACE.

With the outbreak of the War of Rebellion, Mr.
DOUGLASS appears in a new role, that of representative
and leader of his people.

Without embroiling himself with those leaders of the
Abolition movement, for whom he had so profound a
veneration, and to whom the world owes an inextin-
guishable debt of gratitude, he saw their error and
realized, as they did not always, that the trend of events
was toward the liberation of his people.

"The more I saw of Abraham Lincoln," he said in
1866, "the more surely I became convinced that he
was the instrument selected by Divine wisdom for the
liberation of my people, and I determined that no effort

should be lacking on my part to uphold his hands. Many of my friends, many of my own people, differed with me, but to my mind the tendency seemed all the time as clear and evident as the sun in heaven."

Of the details of this time I know but little. That, in the main, Mr. Douglass stood firm in his faith in that man who, as the years go by, is seen more and more clearly to have been in brain, in tact, in unobtrusive steadfastness, in faith and prophetic clearness of vision, the greatest man of his age, if not of any age, — Abraham Lincoln, — there can be no question. That he should sometimes have wavered is not to be wondered at, when Sumner and Wilson, Phillips and Wade, lost faith in the leader whose greatness and wisdom, patience and sagacity, they failed to comprehend.

From the first, Mr. Douglass urged upon the President the employment of colored men, if not as soldiers, at least as organized laborers. As soon as the time was ripe, he began to urge their enlistment as soldiers, and devoted himself to the recruiting and organization of such forces. It is said that one who was urging the organization of colored troops said to Mr. Lincoln: "Why do you not give Fred Douglass a commission?" — "What rank would you suggest?" asked the President. — "Why not make him a brigadier?" was the reply. "He could easily raise a division of colored troops."

"Where would you get the officers?" asked Lincoln. "If Mr. Douglass had a military training and we could find colored men capable of service as field, line, and staff for such a command, it would be different. But you must remember that even then the problem would not be solved. *Mr. Douglass is not a citizen of the United States.* Would I be justified in appointing him to a responsible command? The truth is, he is too big for a small place. He is the representative of his people, and it would not be to their interest that he should hold a subordinate position. I appreciate Mr. Douglass' merit, and he appreciates the difficulties of my position."

"I felt abashed," said my informant, "that I had not realized these difficulties before they were pointed out to me."

There is no doubt that there was a disposition to urge such action upon the President, and if Mr. Douglass had taken counsel of his ambition instead of keeping in view the welfare of his people and the country whose destiny they must share, it is quite probable that such an experiment might have been tried. That it would have been hazardous to the Union cause, the emancipation of the slaves and the fame of Mr. Douglass, there can be little doubt. Without the recognition to which he was so well entitled, and which few men would have foreborne to claim, Mr. Douglass devoted himself to the raising of troops for the defence of the Union.

EMANCIPATION.

At the close of the war, Mr. Douglass found himself in a position of the highest honor and extremest difficulty. By the white people of the North he was regarded as in an especial manner the representative of the colored people. The colored people of the South, only half-informed with regard to his peculiar relation to the long struggle which had culminated in their emancipation, as yet regarded him simply as the most fortunate of his race, whose position in the esteem of the country only showed to what others might attain. They did not realize that during all these years while he had been fighting valiantly the battle of freedom, he had been under a process of education the like of which no other man of his race ever enjoyed. From slavery to the society of men and women of the highest culture in the land; from service under a harsh task-master to being the honored guest in the best white homes of the land, was a transformation few men would have had the moral quality to experience without becoming giddy with an undue sense of their own personal merit. Escaping that, however, such a life was the most perfect of educational forces which swiftly removed him to an infinite distance from the life from which he had fled. He became a slave who had put slavery under his feet. He found himself, in sentiment and feeling, much nearer akin to the most refined white society of the North than to the "freedmen" of the South. They had been freed in an instant. The moral and intellectual stamp of slavery was still upon them. He had had thirty years of preparation for the miracle he lived to behold.

During all this time, his whole thought had been liberty. Freedom for all, equal right before the law; that was all he asked for those akin to him in blood and linked with him in destiny. His mind had never gone beyond this climax. He had never asked himself what would happen afterwards. Until the outbreak of the war,

indeed, he never expected to see this result. He did
not doubt that it would come, but looked upon it as
being generations away rather than close at hand. While
his caution and sense of practicality showed him the
utterly delusive character of John Brown's vision of a
government based on the hope of systematic coöperation
of the slave-population of the South in an endeavor to
destroy slavery by force, yet his despair of better
results under existing conditions was such as to restrain
him from giving information in regard to the same or
approving the desperate venture on which this "inspired
maniac" was about to engage. Had he been able to
forecast even possible success, there is no doubt that
he would have engaged in it most heartily. But he
saw only defeat, useless sacrifice, and the contempt of
all practical people. Brown was angry because he did
not give entire approval to his desperate venture. It
was well that he did not. Its hopelessness was the
very element that gave it strength. That such a little
company should embark upon so desperate a venture
to secure liberty for a despised race, fixed the world's
attention and made the leader's death a grand and
awful spectacle. If he had been in fact, as he desired
and hoped to be, the advance-guard of a popular movement to free the slaves by force of arms, his act would
have been robbed of the moral grandeur on which its
effect depended.

It was not, of course, possible that Mr. DOUGLASS
should foresee such result. The question in his mind was
merely as to its success, and this he at once decided in
the negative. He was willing to engage in anything

that promised good results, no matter how desperate, but would not give his approval to what seemed destined to hinder rather than advance the end he sought.

Emancipation came to him, as to all others, as a surprise. Until the very last moment it was doubtful whether the government would appeal to this extraordinary power in order to put down rebellion. When it was done it was doubtful whether the people of the North would approve. Even if they did approve, it was a question as to what would be the legal result. Not until December, 1865, was the XIIIth Amendment of the Constitution made the law of the land and slavery abolished. Even then, the problem of the future relations of the white and colored man in the American republic was but half-solved — perhaps not even half-solved. Five millions of people who had been slaves were made free by its provisions. Yet they were not citizens. No man could buy or sell them or control their labor for his own advantage; but they had no rights, except such as the several States might confer upon them; they were not citizens, but freedmen, or. in the language of the Chief Justice of the Supreme Court of the United States. in the Dred Scott decision, they were "free persons of color," "mere inhabitants" of the several States, without rights, except such as the States might confer upon them.

It was three years afterward, in July, 1868, when the XIVth Amendment was proclaimed, and for the first time in our history, a colored man became a CITIZEN OF THE UNITED STATES.

During these years the fact developed that mere liberty. the abolition of "slavery and involuntary servitude."

was not enough to secure for the colored man that
equal enjoyment of privilege and opportunity which is the
essence of liberty. It became apparent to all observers
that the long struggle for the abolition of slavery was not
the end of conflict for the establishment and perfection
of the liberty of the individual. The destruction of slavery
had only unmasked the other and more difficult problem
of Caste.

A RACE REDEEMED.

There was something pathetic in the feeling of dis-
appointment which came over Mr. DOUGLASS as he
realized this fact. He had fought so long for liberty,
had hoped for so much, and now it seemed as if
the great conflict for justice had just began. He was
not a leader in the sense of one who devises policies or
methods. He did not originate. His function was to
judge of what others might offer — to pass upon the
practicability of the plans of others. What was needed
to make the work of emancipation and enfranchisement
complete and effectual? This was the question he was
always asking, until the end came. At first he relied on
the provisions of the XIVth Amendment. They seemed
to him sufficient; but as they were bent and twisted,
in the process of legal construction, he gave up that
hope. Of the opinion in the case of the United
States *vs.* Cruikshank, he said pithily: "It is the Dred
Scott case of the new dispensation."

To the clamorous and pathetic appeal of his people
to be delivered from unjust discrimination, from oppression and outrage, which they suffered because of race
and color, he could only answer, "Wait, work, hope!"

It was a vague remedy — how vague he well knew, as those to whom it was addressed fully realized. In this again, that strong and cautious self-restraint which was a marked feature of his character showed itself most clearly. He dreaded above all things giving any advice to his people that might work them injury. He recognized his inability to cope with the new problem. His life-thought had been fixed on liberty. He had studied slavery in all its phases. Caste, the distinction in legal right or opportunity based on race or color and having its root in legislation of a subtle, evasive, and fraudulent character — this was an enemy of a new type. The old arguments would not do. The old weapons were powerless against it. The old allies were dispersed and could not be rallied to fight the new wrong. Other men must be trained for the warfare. Other hands must forge the new weapons. Other hearts must bear the burden. Other souls must endure the scath of the impending conflict. This was the conclusion at which he arrived during the years that lay between emancipation and the time when he was called to give up his work on earth.

Once during the last year of life the old lion roused himself for battle. In the congress in regard to the state and condition of the Negro, held at Chicago during the World's Fair, the old argument of the essential and organic inferiority of the colored race was put forth with almost as much particularity as in the old days when it was made the justification of iniquity and the excuse of oppression. At the sound of this familiar war-cry the old soldier mustered his failing energies, and the torrent of ridicule and denunciation of this infamous standard by which it is still sought to measure his people's right to enjoy "life, liberty, and the pursuit of happiness," is said by those who heard it, to have been worthy of his best estate.

"It is the old, old fight," he said to me a few months afterwards. "The strange claim that a white, intelligent, Christian people makes of right dependent on race or color — of a right to oppress, to degrade, to subjugate, or destroy another people, merely because they are not as white or as wise or as strong as themselves. Will it never end? Will the civilized white man never cease trying to outdo the savage in barbarity? Will the Christian never learn that the colored man is only a weaker brother? God only knows what the end will be! I am waiting — waiting with my ear close to the ground to catch the sound of the chariot wheels!"

REWARDS OF LABOR.

His prominence as a colored man — the fact that he was, indeed, the only colored man known to the whole country — made it eminently proper that he should be recognized by the government which he had served in promoting its most important policy.

When President Grant proposed the acquisition of a naval station in San Domingo, — a proposal which our present complications with England over the Venezuelan boundary and possible complication with Spain growing out of Cuban affairs show to have been

a policy of the highest wisdom, — Mr. DOUGLASS,
with Dr. Howe and Senator Wade, were designated as
a commission to proceed to San Domingo and ascer-
tain and report upon the conditions there prevailing,
and the desirability of such action. It was the first
time a Negro had been charged with any public
function by the government of the United States, and
this action of the great soldier was correctly construed
by the world into a purpose on his part to maintain
the policy and guarantee of equal citizenship for the
colored man, which his party had proclaimed and the
country had indorsed.

He was afterward appointed Marshal of the District
of Columbia, Register of the same, and Minister Plenipotentiary to Hayti. These honors brought also wealth
and the means for enjoying a dignified and well-earned
leisure. For the first time in the history of the
Republic, a Negro became an important and universally
esteemed personage at the capital of the Union. He
was a marked and honored presence at all ceremonial
functions, and was sought out by travellers from all
lands as one of the most notable and distinguished
citizens of the Republic. In all his official relations he
was dignified, courteous, and incorruptible.

He realized the dignity of the position he held
and would not permit any one, however high, to question his rights or reflect upon his fitness or capacity
to discharge its duties. While Minister to Hayti a
naval officer was sent to the island charged with a
diplomatic mission which he was to perform, not in
connection with the Minister, but in disregard of him

and his high office. Mr. DOUGLASS regarded this as
an affront which was put upon him because of his
race, and promptly resigned. He was probably correct
in his conclusion that such a course would never have
been adopted if the Minister Plenipotentiary had been
a white man. At all events, he was right in resenting
it as an affront to himself, and through him to the
people of whom he was the special representative and
exponent.

THE LESSON OF HIS LIFE.

His memory should be an inspiration to every colored
man and a warning to every white American that
caste discrimination, whether it be the prop of slavery
or other wrong, cannot long be justified by its results.
While it may be many years or even generations before
another colored man will attain the same distinctive
prominence in the whole country, Mr. DOUGLASS was
not only the exponent of new conditions but the excep-
tion that proves the rule in regard to old ones. A
people that can produce a DOUGLASS under the conditions that beset his life, will unquestionably produce many
who shall be his superiors in attainment and power
under an improved environment. The law of the evo-
lution of types in humanity is just as inflexible as in
the lower orders of life. One DOUGLASS born out of
slavery is the forerunner of many to be born out of the
semi-freedom which is all that Caste permits his race
yet to enjoy.

The difficulties that beset his life can never be
duplicated in all the world's life which is to be. One

of the twin dragons of oppression has at least been slain. Slavery is no more. From the rising to the setting of the sun there is no place in any civilized land where oppression dare wear that name. The slave-ship, the slave-mart, the auction-block, the life which was in all things subject to another's will, the political condition which denied marriage and family, and legal offspring, which by law refused the rights of self-defence, forbade the race to possess or to inherit; to receive, to give or take; to sue or be sued; which denied the sacred rite of marriage, and in the name of Christ forced millions to an adulterous estate to gratify Christian lust and greed — this monster, which not only had survived the Dark Ages but grew daily more horrible in character and aspect with the advance of civilization, is at least no more! Not only in our land but in all the earth slavery is dead! Only the evil stench of its decay remains to offend the moral sense of man!

Caste, the twin demon, is yet to be destroyed. Let the life of FREDERICK DOUGLASS be an example to those who must take up the conflict where he was obliged to lay it down, and a warning to those who would put aside and cover up the wrongs done to-day, in the name of science and of that new God which measures human rights, not by manhood but by race and color, making the shallow claim of a supreme superiority the excuse for wrong. A nation, a civilization, a Christianity, which within one man's memory upheld slavery with all its horrors should hesitate to proclaim anew its infallibility. The land which gave a million lives to destroy the demon Slavery, should beware of enthroning in its place the fouler and more dangerous Moloch, CASTE!

As slave, freedman, citizen, and patriot, FREDERICK DOUGLASS' life was such as to reflect fame upon his people, credit upon those who listened to his admonitions, renown upon the nation, which finally recognized his merits, and honor on all who do honor to his memory. Within this fane dedicated to liberty and the memory of noble sons of the Republic, no worthier life has been commemorated.

PERSONAL REMINISCENCES

PERSONAL REMINISCENCES OF FREDERICK DOUGLASS.

It is peculiarly fitting that Boston, here in sacred Faneuil Hall, should recognize the talents, admire the wonderful career, and exalt the lofty virtues of one among the most eminent of her adopted and favorite sons. It was upon this free soil of Massachusetts that FREDERICK DOUGLASS, the panting fugitive, first felt secure from the bay of the blood-hounds of slavery.

It was here, alas! he awoke too soon to the fact that not even the Bay State strand, at that time, could really guarantee the liberty and privileges which the Constitution of the United States had promised to her citizens. Here, also, he learned that caste still dared to ostracize where freedom nominally reigned; and that here free locomotion, manly expansion, and full Christian development were not, at that time, considered wholly necessary for those of a black skin.

But, on the other hand, it was Massachusetts — at Lynn, at Nantucket, at Salem, and even in the Boston of that day — who by her very atmosphere, even then rapidly purifying, filled the lungs and roused all the faculties of a great dormant soul.

This of itself is no small renown, even for so great a State. No small plaudit, even for her whose boast still

is that the brightest jewels of her crown are " her sons,
native and adopted, the character, services, and fame of
those who have benefited and adorned their day and
generation."

It was on Massachusetts soil FREDERICK DOUGLASS
laid aside the exhorter's robe, hushed the Baltimore
camp-meeting melodies and Sharpe-street's trumpet-calls
to salvation, and essayed rather to preach the living
gospel, not alone in the freedom of Christ but for the
freedom of humanity.

In the memorable school-house at Nantucket — the
home of great Paul Cuffee, navigator, merchant, colo-
nizer, strenuous always for civil rights, teacher and
upholder of the Friendly Creed — DOUGLASS found at
last his tongue suddenly and miraculously loosened; saw
the blinding light from heaven, streaming in all efful-
gence, lighting up the pathway before him. Here was
his earliest school, the Academy of the Abolitionists, —
that log college of fiery eloquence, fierce dialectic, keen
analysis, and unsparing criticism, — the best equipped of
its day, at once idealistic, realistic, and sternly practical.

To an unusually sensitive soul, to one extraordinarily
attuned and keyed to catch and return the slightest
emotion, everything at this remarkable period conspired
to develop, expand, and stimulate the late slave-boy of the
Chesapeake. Quaker prudence and the "inner light,"
Puritan zeal for right, and Pilgrim faith and trust, the
friendly hand, the beaming, approving eye, the hearty
sympathy which not only recognized a new-found brother,
but resolved he should be heard.

"Though under a roof of black."

The sights, the controversies of the time, historic places, and venerated names, still kept alive in lofty deed and noble aim by honored descendants, — the Sewalls, Quincys, Phillipses, Bowditches, and Pillsburys, heirs of all the past, — all combined to furnish this illustrious fugitive the grandest opportunity for the best instruction. Here was the finest anvil on which to beat into sturdiest strength and deftest symmetry the polished weapons of oratory, persuasion, pathos, humor, and invective.

Bred upon the seashore, trained in the shipyard, having caught glimpses of the eloquence of the ages in the "Columbian Reader;" catching his first full, free breath by "the deep-sounding waves" of Nantucket, can we wonder why FREDERICK DOUGLASS, to his latest day, always turned with full heart, trembling voice, and ever respectful homage at the very name of Massachusetts.

Upon the altar which she long years after raised to defend the integrity of the Union he offered his sons to the glorious Fifty-fourth Massachusetts Volunteers; to the equally meritorious Seventh Massachusetts Cavalry; and took his part in the recruiting service.

Crude in thought, diffident and distrustful of his powers, as I have heard him say, he was really frightened at his first success. He had the rare frankness in later years to acknowledge that his first inspiration to higher effort, to more sustained flights of oratory, and more careful preparation, came from hearing the gifted, eloquent negro, born under the shadows of Harvard, educated at Salem, cultured by travel, and refined by the fortunate circumstances of cultivated friendships and associations — Charles Lenox Remond.

Mr. DOUGLASS used to say that inheriting the prejudices among which he had grown up, there was no surprise in the beginning at Garrison, Quincy, Phillips, and Pillsbury. They were all white men, diverse though they were in culture, and talent, and eloquence. In his mind they were naturally heirs to all the learning of the ages. Hitherto he had heard only the intelligent negro as a fervent exhorter in the religious home, in Sharpe-street Church, Baltimore, wherein he had early sought peace in religion. But the deep feelings, and the untrained, rude language of these men, though freighted with all the fullest and loftiest ideals of Christian truth, yet jarred on his own sensitive and poetic ear, and seemed mere noise and pathos, sincere though it was; it seemed, indeed, to lack the one note for which his soul yearned — cultivation. He had never expected to find it among his own race, and had thought it unattainable until he heard Remond.

He deemed it even then peculiar to New England-reared colored men, until in the national convention of colored citizens, held at Buffalo, N.Y., August 15, 1843, where Remond, of Salem, and DOUGLASS, of Boston, represented Massachusetts, he listened for the first time to other educated, talented, and intrepid colored men, preachers, teachers, business men, scholars, and specialists — Wright, Ray, Garnet, Beaman, Platt, Johnson, Loguen, Malvin, Francis, and others, whose friendship there begun, he enjoyed, in some instances, for over forty years. Many persons, even now more unfamiliar with the true history of the negro in America than Mr. DOUGLASS was then, are inclined to look upon him as the only intellectual, the only eloquent orator, debater, and writer among his race; but at no time of his wonderful and varied career did any one hear him even intimate, much less make, such an assertion.

I remember hearing him say of the venerated Bishop Loguen that he was "one of the most powerful orators" he had ever heard; of Garnet, that he was "a master of invective;" of Ringgold Ward, that "his eloquence was as intense as his blackness," and "his gestures as graceful as his body was huge and ungainly;" of Remond, "I always kept him in mind, and became almost wild when I read of his wonderful speeches in Exeter Hall."

So Themistocles was kept awake by the fame of the illustrious dead of the Ceramicus. So genius ever needs the stimulus of recorded deeds, or the hoof-beat of the pacer, the snort of a rival, or the indefinable electric presence of kindred genius, to rouse to highest effort.

As a Boston boy, I well recall my first sight of Mr. DOUGLASS in the late fifties. It was in the old Melodeon, on Washington street, where the Anti-Slavery conventions and Woman's Rights conventions were wont to be held.

I had been accustomed to read FREDERICK DOUGLASS' paper "The North Star," but was too young to have formed any clear notion of his personality. Through the kindness of my mentor and early friend, William C. Nell, whose statue of Attucks — his life's dream — is at last, thank God, erected, I was privileged to go to the rear of the stage entrance and there for the first time saw in one group, DOUGLASS, Garrison, Abby Kelly Foster, Purvis, Sojourner Truth, Phillips, Pillsbury, and William Wells Brown.

To-night memory brings back the vision of Æschines in exile, reading Demosthenes on the Crown to his rapt pupils, "would that you could have seen, would that you could have heard the great original." To my boyish sight Mr. DOUGLASS appeared even taller and brawnier of frame then than any of those about him, and often afterwards I was inclined to think it the natural exaggeration of youth; but recently having come across the photograph of the Santo-Domingo Commission, where Mr. DOUGLASS is seen seated at the left of the Commissioners, on the deck of the man-of-war, the same physical superiority there manifest confirms my earliest impression. Several generations must have combined to produce that frame of rugged oak, as centuries must have rolled by and many climes conjoined to have produced that subtlety of mind, and those exquisite effects of voice, of tone, so rich in its cadent swell, that resembled what may seem a trite, but the only applicable, metaphor, the rolling of the billows on the shore, the booming of the sea beyond.

This first meeting with him brings out only the central figure and that historic anti-slavery group. There was a clash of opinion, all I at present recall, and Sojourner Truth, slender, black, weird, seeress in speech and manner — sibyl, indeed, a fit foil to DOUGLASS — was opposed; but it was the fencing of the representatives, man and woman, of the black race.

Afterward, at the Annual Bazaars, at the Twelfth

Baptist Church, where he lectured, and on the first anniversary of the hanging of John Brown, when a Boston mayor tried to put down free speech, and occasioned Wendell Phillips' finest effort. "Mobs and Education." I had an opportunity to see, to know, to enjoy his personal friendship, and reverently study the manifold phases of his unique character.

In 1859–60 every Massachusetts breeze was surcharged with the elixir of liberty. My recollections of that time relate to places, men, and scenes — to Philiips' "Toussaint L'Ouverture" at Mercantile Hall; Theodore Parker's and Emerson's discourses at Music Hall, on Sundays; Frank Sanborn, J. Sella Martin, Redpath, O'Connor, and Hinton; Higginson, Bowditch, Merriam, Whipple, and "The Traveller," Slack and "The Commonwealth," Z. K. Pangborn and our grandest Governor, John A. Andrew. One felt and knew that the contest was on; that the era of moral suasion had passed; that there was a Spartan band on Massachusetts soil determined to grapple at once with slavery and fight it to the death.

The meeting of the 3d December, 1860, was too large for the lesser temple, the Meionaon, where Emerson and the Woman's Rights advocates were wont to hold forth. It was adjourned to the larger temple above, so historically sacred to free discussion.

I was there, and had edged my way near my friends, Sella Martin and FREDERICK DOUGLASS, at the side platform, just as the howling mob swept into the hall and took possession.

Not an Abolitionist retreated. On the contrary,

Richard J. Hinton, known then to me by sight and
name, called me to him, asked if I knew where Redpath's office was, and bade me take this card I now
hold up, a sacred relic, to that office and bring back
John Brown's revolver.

Mr. DOUGLASS said "Go;" Mr. Martin said "Go;"
but I needed no second admonition. Inspired by the
errand, I ran and brought the revolver under my jacket,
and remained on the platform beside Mr. DOUGLASS
until the hall was cleared; but the card I have religiously
preserved as a memento of a day few Bostonians now
feel proud to recall. There is a compensation, it is
said, in every untoward event. On that gloomy
night, when free speech seemed stifled in the city of
Boston, where were Sanborn, Phillips, DOUGLASS, and
Hinton forced to seek and find relief? In the old ark
of safety on Joy street, the ancient church of Rev.
Nathaniel Paul, co-worker with Garrison in England,
the same building wherein the Massachusetts Anti-
Slavery Society drew its first breath, a church then
presided over by the eloquent J. Sella Martin. Here
the Abolitionists met, while the mob raged without,
and celebrated the martyrdom of John Brown. Here
they got their second wind for the conflict already
precipitated.

The war came. Mr. Phillips spoke for the first time
"under the flag." We know how Mr. DOUGLASS
threw himself all heart and mind and soul into that
conflict; with what enthusiasm he and the Disunionists,
the Abolitionists, and the Republicans, and the Demo-
crats, too, at last rallied together for the defence of the

Union, which meant to all a land free without a slave — the ideal Republic.

I was at school at Oberlin during the battle years 1862–1863, and hence did not hear him, as some here to-night heard him when Judge Russell ran up the steps of the platform of that same Tremont Temple bringing the despatch that Abraham Lincoln had issued the Proclamation of Freedom! What a coincidence! From the very spot whence he had been driven 1860, the great FREDERICK DOUGLASS gave the words to that waiting, anxious audience, "Praise God from whom all blessings flow," and the vast throng joined in the grand Benediction.

I stood in Faneuil Hall, however, when the surrender at Appomattox came, and heard Rue's swelling song of Jubilee; heard shouts of victory, and those Union choruses since known everywhere. The stentorian notes of our greatest orator, great man, lover of his race, but greater lover of humanity, sounded forth the praises of the Great Ulysses, captain of armies, the silent man of American history, whose fame, now trumpet-tongued, has swept over the world.

Who can ever forget that scene? We seemed then to be living — we were living — in an heroic age, when words were deeds, and deeds were crystallized into everlasting principles; when men seemed likest gods, living, acting, breathing, and contending not for self, nor place, nor power, not to rivet chains, but to strengthen for all time the freedom of their country.

Party, faction, race, for once, at least, in America were in reality lost sight of; for once slavery, caste, rebellion found no defender, no apologizer throughout the length and breadth of the reunited nation, and on such occasion, brief, alas! brief as it was, the great orator whom we mourn to-night rose perhaps to the transcendent height of his aspiration and his fame.

That was an exultant hour; too rapturous to last! Grave, grave, grave indeed is the responsibility of the reactionists who began from that night the propaganda to regain, on the field of diplomacy, what they had lost in the wager of battle; to relegate to *quasi-peonage* the slaves whom war and military necessity had freed.

Thirty years have passed since that eventful night; thirty years of vast national progress in wealth, of philanthropic effort; years marked in science and education; in the restoration of the negro's right to suffrage; in the industrial development of the great mass of the former bondmen; but with all the progress, all the education, thrift, patient endurance, and deferred hope, the disgraceful fact remains, and the sacred cause of truth requires it to be solemnly said here in Faneuil Hall that FREDERICK DOUGLASS was untimely cut off, through zeal, shame, indignation, and righteous wrath at the barbarities perpetrated upon his race by men indebted to them for citizenship; at the unpardonable indifference of Northern Christians, so solicitous for the woes of far-off Armenians; at the slow-footed American justice; at the sheathed sword of national authority, which flashes not forth like the mailéd arm of this Commonwealth, nor utters its time-honored and ever-respected injunction :

Manus haec inimica tyrannis,
Ense petit placidam, sub libertate quietem.

FREDERICK DOUGLASS undoubtedly died heart-broken at the farce of freedom, the travesty of American citizenship, in the late rebellious States, and worn out with speaking and writing, with the fervor of fifty years before.

Some of you saw him a year ago at Providence, at that meeting where I had the honor to preside. We saw then the handwriting on the wall.

It is not enough for us here to repeat the marvellous story of his life. No one will ever tell it with more simplicity, more heart-stirring pathos, than he himself has already done in matchless prose, worthy of the simple annals of the Scotch peasantry. We are not here to praise his eloquence, much less describe it. We know that it is not lost to the world, but is already coursing upon a thousand precious-laden breezes; has already swept over the entire land, and has touched the hearts and lips, and fired the unconquerable souls of a thousand black Douglasses, not so eminent, perhaps, as their great exemplar, but resolved, from the rapt fervor of his latest exhortation — to take up his unfinished work; the vindication of the complete, indefeasible, unextinguishable citizenship of the American negro, at this present moment in greater jeopardy than it was even before Bull Run.

It is customary to speak of Mr. DOUGLASS as a great negro, and to dismiss the race to oblivion, by scanty accorded and only partial justice even to him. He was a great man judged by any standard, of any

race, at any time, in this world's history. Like his
prototype, Alexandre Dumas, *père*, whom he resembled
only in genius, he will rank among Nordau's great
men of the world. Like the great Irish agitator,
O'Connell, whom he so much resembled in many
respects, he was at once typical of the highest char-
acteristics of the races whose mingled blood flowed
through his veins.

He was truly, as no white man could be, the typical,
composite American, for in his veins there flowed,
without a doubt, the negro, the indian, the white
strain of stock, and I always suspected a touch of
that Berber blood whose fire and genius in every southern State has helped to save the native African from
the extreme cruelty of the Anglo-Saxon.

There was a world of deep philosophy in a remark
made by him when he was unjustly and unduly criti-
cised by some negroes, "I am not a negro; look at
my features; look at my hair."

He was not, it is true, a pure negro in blood; such
was the ethnological fact; that, however, was not
necessary either to assert his full claim to recognition
as a man and an American citizen, nor could the fact
disparage his intellect, or lessen the deep interest he
always felt in his mother's race. Had she not been
the guiding star of his childhood, though seen only at
night, like the fabric of a vision? Did there not always
sing in his soul the mystical sounds crooned to him
in the lonely watches, — words the childish mind could
not comprehend, which, perhaps, his maturer manhood
even never wholly fathomed.

He resented the idea that an unknown father should lay claim to his intellect, and we know to-day, thanks to heredity and science, that in intellect and in feeling, in lofty aspiration, in uncommon good-sense, in wondrous depths of humor, he was a true mother-child.

Did he know much of grief in all that strange, eventful life? Many think not, because he did not wear it on his sleeve. The devoted wife of his early days, faithful companion, suggester and companion of his flight, who combined, as some of us know, the tenderest qualities of wife, mother, and friend, left at her death a void in the heart of her husband and of every friend who knew her intimately.

Mr. DOUGLASS mourned her as the husband mourns the true wife, as the wife mourns the devoted husband; the pain that numbs and deadens, from which we rise to life, with a slower step and a lessened ardor; but the greatest grief of Mr. DOUGLASS' life, known only to his most intimate friends, indeed sacredly guarded as a vestal fire from the profane, came to him earlier in life — it was the loss of his favorite daughter, Annie, the apple of his eye, the one clinging plant of that middle-life, his own image in the opposite sex; the transmission and the cross, which perpetuates genius, the heart which, above all others, he ever knew, responded most completely to every note and tone of his own soul's harmony.

For years no one dared to mention her to him, except when he was alone; while the souvenirs of her precocity, her extreme sensibility, and her mobile and radiant

nature, were a perennial source of comfort at times of
political distrust, of personal misrepresentation, of mis-
understanding.

In the summer of 1868 he invited me, a college
student, to visit him at his home in Rochester, in
the old house well remembered by so many of
his intimate friends of that day. Here with his violin,
his books, and collection of English scenes and memen-
toes, a new side of his nature was revealed, a side ever
ready to swing wide its portal, but always requiring
a sympathetic touch to move the springs. It was on
this visit I saw the relics of the daughter gone, and
there learned the wondrous hold she had upon his
whole being.

He had fled to England, on the opening of the
John Brown investigation, which meant evidently hanging for such as were proved cognizant of the hero's
plans. Ordinarily, she would have accompanied her
father; but his safety demanded prudence. She literally pined away with grief during his absence, and the
uncertainty of its duration, never having been sepa-
rated from him before; and she died at the budding
of womanhood, with a plaintive call for the absent
father last on her lips.

Honors came, many and greater than his fondest
dreams could have imagined; brighter even than the
boyish visions by the shores of the Chesapeake when
the "slave-ships" sailed by; and the bright clouds
illumined by gorgeous, dazzling sunlight used to conjure
up visions worthy of the Apocalypse. No honor, however, came too high nor undeserved; none that did not

have the bitter dreg of American prejudice thrown in to poison the cup; but neither the honors nor the dregs of the chalice ever were able to make him forget the one hand nor gave so lasting a pang as this worst grief.

It has been a matter of surprise to some persons that a man of Mr. DOUGLASS' physique and moral courage should have had, as he freely confessed, such a dread, daily, hourly, on his escape from bondage, of capture; that he should have fled to England, alarmed and dreading the Fugitive Slave Law. The explanation has ever seemed to me simple, not from any remark dropped from him, but rather from an analysis of his peculiarly remarkable organization. He was essentially a sensitive, in spite of his sturdy, physical organization. In truth, a more highly developed sensitive, from the very combination of massive frame and delicacy of mind. He should have been able, as he was, to strike the lowest and the highest notes, and be alive to the varied strokes in turn, roused or depressed to an extent which less acutely organized beings cannot comprehend.

The horrible thought and fact of slavery had become so abhorrent to him, so cumulative and harrowing in the quick tense vibrations of his thought, that they certainly would have beat higher and higher, and in time overbalanced his reason, had the dread been permitted to remain, or had the cloud not been lifted.

He was essentially a man of peace, and naturally took to "non-resistance," the peaceful method of agitation of the Society of Friends, whose interest in him never allowed its Light to grow dim, and to whom he owed much that is unrecorded.

At the convention of 1843 he was the consistent opponent of the fiery Garnet and others, advising the torch and physical resistance. We know now he never favored Brown's plan as developed, and his opposition, as early as 1843, and as late as 1859, yes, and 1893, when plans were set on foot to apply the *lex talionis* in lynching matters, his arguments, precedents, and boundless faith, in all probability, prevented much bloodshed.

This aversion to force, and horror of even abstract oppression, this frenzy of speech at all species of wrong, arose, as can easily be imagined, from a nature capable of the widest outbursts of feeling, the outcome of which in more peaceful times would have been in the highest degree poetic.

I have often conjectured whether or not his thought ever took on this form; that the potency was there, is seen in his speeches and in a venture of his, which I only discovered by chance, a story, " Madison Washington," written with all the gracefulness of his best estate, a story needing only time and elaboration to have made it a study of negro character worthy of later times and his maturer years.

He never referred to it in my hearing; perhaps he was ashamed of this youthful venture. He need not have discarded this early literary offspring, for in plot, conception, and delineation it was worthy of its author, and the theme.

Mr. DOUGLASS has always been spoken of as the natural, " self-made " orator; but with me there has always been present, in everything that Mr. DOUGLASS wrote, the unconscious trace, an odor of the lamp, one always well filled, well trimmed too, and kept brightly burning. I find this as conspicuous in his lectures on American slavery (Buffalo, 1851) as in the Lessons of the Hour (A. M. E. "Church Review," July, 1894).

He seemed to have the grand Miltonic scorn of coming into a contest of thought unprepared; with his blade not well sharpened, the hilt untried, and the point not tested. I dare assert, judged by any papers of eminent American statesmen, writers, or even lawyers, arguing from precedent, case, or analogy, Mr. DOUGLASS will be found never to have been careless in the form of his thought, never negligent in his method, and almost invariably accurate and even elegant in choice and application of words; while some of his aphorisms are worthy of Victor Hugo himself, and will live in American literature. "One, with God, is a majority;" "The Republican party is the ship, all outside is the sea;" "In American law the slave has no wife, no children, no country, no home;" "Slavery is always slavery; always the same foul, [illegible] damning scourge;" "There comes no voice from the enslaved;" "The Irishman is poor, but he is not a slave;" "I began to pray with my legs;" "When men prefer the crooked to the straight road, it is not because the one is crooked and the other is straight, but because of some fancied advantage apart from the character of the roads themselves;" "Mankind seems fated to find Truth only through a howling wilderness of Error. The wonder is less that they have gone wrong, than that they have gone right at all. On first view, Error would seem to have everything its own way, opening wide its thousand gates against the single one of Truth. .   By some means or other, whatever may be said in favor of the doctrine of innate depravity, men do and will in the end prefer truth to error, right to wrong."

If my claim is well founded, it should dispose of the semi-disparagement which makes mere oratorical emotion the greatest strength, and fails to estimate the greater glory which comes from a trained intellect wielding the mightiest of weapons.

Those who only knew Mr. DOUGLASS as the bitter opponent of slavery, the picturesque and typical negro, Marshal of the District of Columbia, Recorder of Deeds, and diplomat, saw only some milder phases of his varied nature. Once, amid the Blue Ridge of Virginia, we were invited to address an emancipation celebration of colored people, gathered from several counties. It was a characteristic scene amid the heights of Virginia, — rural, jovial, eminently Southern in its types and scenes, — all that goes to make up the negro's personality, not omitting his proverbial good nature and superabundant vitality.

Mr. DOUGLASS was not entirely at ease on this occasion; his mind was in the mountains and far away, so he turned me in, as he said, " to do the hard work." By the time I had finished he was strolling leisurely, viewing the romantic scene, finding his way at last over the ground to a carriage the occupants of which had beckoned to him. They proved to be old friends: one, the patriarch, a Pennsylvania Quaker, who had known him years before. We were invited to the ancient homestead, — the earliest drift southward of the Penn stock, —

dating back to the seventeenth century, and there for the first time in years I saw Mr. Douglass at his best estate, at once entertainer and entertained, witty, learned, aphoristic, epigrammatic, bubbling over with brilliant sayings, quotations; radiantly happy among cultivated, appreciative auditors; felicitous in expression, and literally flashing with quaint, humorous, and serious reminiscences, just as some brown Brahmin shines in cultivated Boston or New York society. And so it was ever with him. His oratory was never conversational, except in tone, for it was the oratory of his youth; but his conversation, when at his best, was the perfection of speech of the true orator. And yet this man, whom the impartial critic will rank among the five truly great men of this country, could say of himself:

"More than twenty years of my life were consumed in a state of slavery. My childhood was environed by the baneful peculiarities of the slave system. I grew up to manhood in the presence of this hydra-headed monster, not as a master, not as an idle spectator, not as a guest of the slave-holder, but as *a slave*, eating the bread and drinking the cup of slavery with the most degraded of my brother bondmen, and sharing with them all the painful conditions of their wretched lot."

And this American slave, whose freedom was ransomed with a price; who attained next to the highest honors of his race; the trusted friend of Abraham Lincoln; the friend, also, of General Grant; orator, office-holder, statesman, and diplomat, — never became in sober truth a real citizen of the United States, so far as the rights, the "privileges," so far as locomotion was concerned; not near so much a true citizen as the slave of Epaphroditus, to whom Judge Tourgée has referred, was in the days of heathen Rome.

FINAL PROCEEDINGS

FINAL PROCEEDINGS.

On the sixteenth of January, 1896, Councilman STANLEY RUFFIN introduced the following resolutions at the meeting of the Common Council, and they were adopted by a unanimous vote; namely:

Resolved, That the thanks of the City Council be hereby expressed to the Hon. ALBION W. TOURGÉE for the eloquent oration delivered by him at the memorial services in honor of the late FREDERICK DOUGLASS, held under the auspices of the city at Faneuil Hall, December 20, 1895.

Resolved, That the thanks of the City Council be hereby expressed to RICHARD T. GREENER, Esq., for the address delivered by him at the memorial services in honor of the late FREDERICK DOUGLASS, at Faneuil Hall, December 20, 1895.

Resolved, That the thanks of the City Council be hereby expressed to the Rev. D. P. ROBERTS for officiating as chaplain at the memorial services in honor of the late FREDERICK DOUGLASS, held by the city in Faneuil Hall, December 20, 1895.

The Board of Aldermen concurred with the Common Council in the adoption of the resolutions, at their meeting, January the twentieth, and the resolutions were approved by the Mayor on the twenty-second of January, 1896.

www.ingramcontent.com/pod-product-compliance
Lightning Source LLC
Chambersburg PA
CBHW020026030726
47499CB00007B/2285